Kin

'"The waters were real dark. I felt spooked. I got checked through security and swam on to the studio. The place looked deserted. I couldn't see any sign of life. No lights on anywhere. I wasn't sure quite where I was meant to be heading.

'Suddenly, I had company. I froze in my fin-prints when I got a look at the fish who'd joined me. It was a big shark – and I mean big."'

Also by Robert Lee
in Magnet paperbacks

Fishy Business
Microfish
The Nervous Wreck

ROBERT LEE

King Conger

Illustrated by Caroline Holden

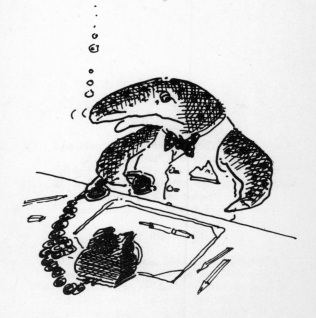

A Magnet Book

First published in 1987
by Methuen Children's Books Ltd
This Magnet paperback edition first published 1989
by Methuen Children's Books
A Division of OPG Services Ltd
Michelin House, 81 Fulham Road, London SW3 6RB
Printed in Great Britain
by Cox & Wyman Ltd, Reading

ISBN 0 416 54630 7

Dedicated to John Krivine,
*hoping that he can placate
those sandy waters....*

Contents

The Cast of Characters

Rock Salmon	*Private Detective*
Sanderson	*His faithful Pilotfish*
Angel Sweetlips	*A fish in a billion*
Ronnie Scuba	*Owner of 'Ronnie Scuba's Dive'*
Hercule Poisson	*Chief Inspector at Intergill*
Cong alias Inimus	*Monster of the Deep*
DinoCod	*Monster of the Deep*
Profish	*Monster of the Deep*
The Great Regnoc	*Monster of the Deep*
Greatwhiteosaurus Rex	*Monster of the Deep*
Sundry Monsters of the Deep	
Dr Ray Thornback	*A scientist*
Professor October	*An eminent scientist*
Cecil Goldfish	*The Movie Mogul*
Art Hake	*The Movie Director*
Salmon Davis	*Rock's nephew*
Ethel Mermaid	*The singer*
The Starfish Sisters	*Great dancers, honestly*
Colefish	*The sports commentator*
Nurse Iceberg	*A Nurse Shark*
Mako The Micky	*A Mako Shark*
An archaeologist who's forgotten his name	

Assorted fish of all shapes and sizes too fishy to mention. . . .

Prefish

The Precific Ocean is unknown to Man and un-
manned by Fish – at least by fish as we know
them. Very few fish in the marine city of Atlantis
had ever heard of the Precific Ocean, let alone
knew where it was.

Among those who had heard mention of these
weird and wonderful waters, strange rumours
abounded. Two famous writers had even written
about the place. Lewis MacCarol spoke of it as a
place where everything is double: 'For in those
seas the sand is twice as sandy, the fish twice as
fishy, and the waters twice as wet . . .'

Sir Isaac Newt agreed with this basic 'double
vision' idea, but from a slightly different view-
point: 'Verily in the Precific Ocean the creatures
are twice as big as double. Indeed, the whales on
the Hippopotamus equal the sum of the fish on the
other two tides.' He put his theory into a formula
for those enlightened enough to understand:–

$$w\left(\xi^2 - \frac{E}{49}\right) = M + M - T$$

with 2 lumps, please.

Inimus had never read anything by Lewis Mac-Carol or Isaac Newt. If the truth be known, he'd never read anything. Why? Because he had spent all of his short life living in the Precific Ocean, a sea so primitive that none of its creatures could read or write.

Inimus was a real live monster of the deep. A giant conger eel more than three times the size of any fish in Atlantis, he would strike terror into anyone from that city who happened to bump into him on a wet afternoon.

Inimus, however, had a problem. Although by Atlantis standards he was a giant, in his home waters he was considered to be quite the opposite. He was surrounded by fellow congers far bigger than he. He was the smallest eel around, and he was never allowed to forget it. What a cruel blow to be called Inimus – only a nickname, his real name was Cong.

Despite his size, Inimus was in a particularly happy mood as he sat inside his cave watching his father – The Great Regnoc – doodling on the wall. For the first time in his life, he had made a friend – another misfit in the waters of the Precific Ocean.

As Inimus sat in his cave, this friend wafted gently and alone just below the surface of the water. He was an extremely smelly fish, and very unpopular. DinoCod – for this was the name of the strange prehistoric fish – accepted his fate, even though it wasn't his fault that he smelt so bad. But he was very glad to have made a friend in Inimus. It was natural that these two outsiders should strike up their friendship. Fish of a gill fit the bill, as the old marine saying goes.

'What think of painting?' asked The Great Regnoc.

Inimus was deep in his thoughts, and failed to hear the question. His father swam into a fury, and scuffed him across the head with his tail.

'Eeeeeeekh,' yelled Inimus. He wasn't really

frightened of his father's terrible temper; he just always made 'eeeeeeekh' noises when he got scuffed. What he was thinking actually bore no resemblance to an 'eeeeeekh' at all. It was more of a 'here goes Dad on his physical aggro trip again' than an 'eeeeeekh'.

'What think of paint?' persisted Regnoc.

'Your best so far, Dad,' he replied quickly. But here again, words bore no resemblance to thoughts. Inimus and everyone else knew that Regnoc was a seriously bad painter.

'Ugh,' agreed Regnoc, content with his son's sensible response.

In Inimus's opinion, 'Ugh' was the truest thing his father had said all day, and was a very good description of his work. If anyone from Atlantis had seen it, he would have thought it so primitive that it had to be of artistic value. Obviously Regnoc had never seen the work of Bottishelli.

Inimus didn't have any interest in his father's work. As soon as Regnoc absorbed himself once more in his brushes, the small giant monster of the deep escaped from the cave and swam towards the surface in search of his friend, DinoCod. . . .

1 · My Fair Fish

The sea has many secrets. No creature alive or dead, wet or dry, has ever fully come to terms with its untamable spirit, its great mystery. As a wise philosophish once said, salt water runs deep.

And so does Sebastian Cod, thought Angel Sweetlips, as she sat glued to the athletics on the television in her new apartment in Lagoon Drive, Atlantis.

It was with a contented sigh that she turned off the television set after watching the great athlete winning yet another memorable race. She had to get ready. She was going to the theatre that evening with Rock Salmon.

Rock Salmon, Private Investigator, had never been much of an Art Shark; in fact, he wasn't a shark at all. He hadn't been to the theatre since his school days, and Angel was surprised when he'd phoned to tell her he had two ringside seats for *My Fair Fish*.

Perhaps the fact that the tickets were free –

courtesy of Rock's nephew, Salmon Davis – had something to do with it. Sam (as Rock's nephew was called) was apparently one of the stars of the show, along with the dazzling Ethel Mermaid.

Angel knew that Rock was not altogether looking forward to the show. Never mind; culture was good for the soul *and* the dogfish. She was slightly grateful that no one had heard her make such a dreadful pun – the kind of line Rock would have come up with, she commented under her bubbles.

They arrived at the theatre with two minutes to spare before the curtain went up and made it to their seats in the nick of time. The lights dimmed at once and the orchestra started to play the opening number.

Up went the curtain and on swam the Starfish Girls, linked together in formation, kicking out their legs in time with the music. With their sequin-spangled silk stockings on every leg, they made quite a splash with the audience.

There was great applause as the conductor whipped the orchestra up towards the climax and Ethel Mermaid dived on stage. She and the Girls swam straight into the opening song:

> *'Swim and the world swims with you.*
> *Under an Ocean of blue . . .'*

It was good stuff.

Soon the Starfish Girls danced off stage. Ethel sang a rather dull song about a piece of jewellery her guy had just given her, and something about coral being a girl's best friend – or words to that effect.

Angel noticed that Rock was beginning to drift off, and she nudged him sharply in the dorsal fin. He sat up with a start.

'What . . .? Where . . .?' he cried.

'Shhh . . .' uttered an officious fish in the row behind.

Angel was deeply embarassed, and apologized on the detective's behalf.

Rock was not enjoying himself. The whole thing was so precious. Why did everyone have to pretend they were enjoying this rubbish? He hated all 'Art Sharks'. Why couldn't they have some nice easy fun songs – like 'Swim and the World Swims With You?'

'Swim and the world swims with you,' sang the Starfish Girls.

And suddenly Rock's nephew, Salmon Davis, was onstage giving his all. He and Ethel sang a duet and tailed their way across the stage. Gradually, the plot began to unfold. Ethel was a fish from the wrong side of town who was in love with Sam, who was from the right side of town and who was equally in love with Ethel.

19

The plot was quaintly old-fashioned. There is no such thing in Atlantis as a wrong or a right side of town. All fish live in harmony in that enlightened community.

Rock was beginning to enjoy himself. Even so, he'd had a hard day and soon managed to fall asleep again. He woke up to the sound of hysterical applause. He had obviously missed the whole thing. Angel was out of her seat and cheering with the best of them. Rock felt duty-bound to join in.

Angel was furious with Rock. Bad enough that he had fallen asleep, he had apparently snored his way through the interval as well. Angel gave him a real earful as they swam backstage to see Sam.

Despite the fact that bees do not live under the sea, there was a hive of activity backstage. Angel and Rock had to inch their way through a fish school of school fish queuing up outside the stage door, with pens and autograph books at the ready, waiting for the stars to emerge. Angel was even asked for her autograph, which she couldn't resist giving.

'How could you?' asked Rock. 'What gives you the right?'

'You're just jealous because they didn't ask you,' she replied, digging him in the dorsal fin with a grin.

Once inside, she and Rock were directed to Salmon Davis' dressing room. Someone had beaten them to it. They found Rock's nephew in conversation with a very flashy fish, dressed up to the gills and wearing a gleaming pearl fin pin.

'. . . And you're just what we're looking for', the flashy fish was saying. 'You'll be great in the part, I kid you not. You'll float through it. You'll be fish dish of the day. And the movie? It'll be a blockbuster. Who's fishing for compliments? Me? Pull the other fin. Do you know who we've got to direct it?'

Before Sam could say 'Art Hake,' the flashy fish replied: 'Art Hake!'

'Holy fish!' uttered Sam.

'Almost, almost.' The fish paused reverently. Although Art Hake was actually a very small fish – a herring – he was a very big film director. 'Anyway, the studio will be in touch. Let me just say once again, you were great tonight. Swim you soon.'

And without so much as acknowledging Angel's and Rock's presence, the flashy fish swam out of the dressing room.

'Who was that?' asked Rock, ever the detective.

'You don't know?' Sam was amazed at his uncle's ignorance.

'Only the greatest film producer in Holly-weed,' announced Angel.

Rock was none the wiser. He liked movies well enough, but he was not well up on people in the

21

movie business.

'Who *is* the greatest film producer in Holly-weed?' he asked.

'Why, Cecil Goldfish, of course,' said Sam, and if he'd had any shoulders, he would have given them an impatient shrug.

'Oh, yes, I've heard of him,' Rock acknowledged.

'The point is, he wants Sam in one of his movies,' said Angel. 'This calls for a celebration. Come on, Rock, we're all going out on the town.'

'Sure,' agreed Rock, always up for a good splash. 'And I know just the place. I've been wanting to go there for some time. You know, Angel – that new club with sole music and lasers. What's it called?'

'You don't mean the Hippodrown?' asked Sam. If the truth be known, he was sometimes a little worried about his Uncle Rock. Wasn't he too old to be splashing around in discos. 'Are you sure you're up to it?' he asked.

'What do you mean?' Rock was genuinely offended.

'Well, I remember you telling me that last time you went to a disco, you pulled a muscle.'

Rock exhaled an embarassed bubble. Angel ignored Sam's comment, but suggested they go down to Ronnie Scuba's Dive and listen to some jazz. The clarinettist Acker Welk was on that night.

No sooner said than swum. Within half an hour they were seated at Rock's favourite table in his favourite club.

2 · Thornback

Ronnie Scuba's Dive was packed to overflowing
for Acker Welk's visit. He'd had a hit years before
with a ballad – 'Strangers Under Shore'. Ever
since, he pulled a large crowd wherever he played
– not that he restricted his repertoire to ballads of
course. He really specialized in dance music.

When Angel Sweetlips and Co. arrived, the
club was in full swim. The dance floor was packed
to overflowing with Atlantis' jazz fans, including,
much to Rock's surprise, Chief Inspector Hercule
Poisson. This official keeper of the peace in Atlantis was more often to be found in his gentlemen's
club playing a gentle game of backsalmon. But
here he was now swinging his tail away on the
dance floor of Ronnie Scuba's Dive with a partner
whom Rock did not recognize.

As a matter of courtesy, he waved at the Chief
Inspector, who reciprocated. Angel, meanwhile,
had managed to arrange a table with the kind help
of the club's owner, Ronnie Scuba himself. They

all sat down, ordered drinks, and made themselves comfortable.

Rock Salmon was a Peeping Tom. He couldn't help it. After all, it was his job to keep his eyes open. He had no desire to dance, but preferred to sit back in the packed club and observe the goings on.

There were all kinds of fish down at Ronnie's that evening: there always were – that's why it was such a success. Big, small, fat, thin, ugly, beautiful – they all swam on down to The Dive.

The only fish Rock knew who didn't tend to frequent the place was his tiny assistant, Sanderson. His idea of a good time was a trip down to the Gluggenheim Art Gallery or Phinharmonic Hall. So there was no trace of *him* in Ronnie's tonight. Come to think of it, Sanderson was such a discreet kind of fish that even if he were there, you still couldn't be sure of the fact.

What Rock *was* sure about was that there was one table in the club occupied by some very strange fellows. There were four of them, trying to look inconspicuous, but sitting bolt upright in their chairs and looking like fish out of water.

'Look at that crowd,' Rock commented.

'Isn't one of them Ray Thornback?' asked Sam.

'Not the explorer?' Angel was intrigued, and spent the next half hour staring.

Ray Thornback was a curious fish. He'd become

a household name in Atlantis a few years back after he'd been the first fish to interview a human being. The interview was broadcast on TV. There were many in Atlantis who thought this interview was faked. Sanderson was convinced of the fact, and that the so-called Dr Thornback was a fraud. Rock had made some enquiries at the time, trusting in Sanderson's intuition, but had drawn a blank.

Angel Sweetlips knew one thing: Ray Thornback had style. There was no getting around that. He stood out in a crowd. She wondered what he was doing in Ronnie Scuba's Dive. Who were his strange companions? She decided to find out.

Making an excuse to go to the lady's room, she made a wide detour around the club so that she could swim past Thornback's table. As she did so, she eavesdropped on the conversation.

'... get to the Precific Ocean through the Straits of Bad Luck? Maybe, maybe.' These words were spoken by a shrill fish with big boggly eyes.

'Shh!' interrupted Thornback, as he became aware of Angel's presence. 'Can I help you, ma'am?' he said with a flashing smile. Angel caught his eye and blushed.

'Er, thank you, no.' She plucked up her courage. 'Aren't you Ray Thornback?'

'That's right. and you are ...?'

'Angel Sweetlips. Pleased to meet you. I'm a great admirer of your work.'

Thornback seemed genuinely pleased.

'Thank you, Ms Sweetlips,' he replied. 'And what line of work are you in?'

'I'm not working at the moment.'

'A girl like you shouldn't need to work for a living,' said Thornback with a grin.

Angel gave the explorer one of her steeliest looks. What did he mean? Why shouldn't she need to work?

'Listen, Dr Thornback, I'm a fully qualified marine scientist, and I'm not working now because my previous employer, Arthur Codswallop, has retired from his job as Minister for Energy. I'm taking a rest.'

'Hey, hey. No offence meant, I can assure you.' His face was suddenly serious. 'How would you like to work for me?'

Angel felt uneasy. Was Thornback on the level? Or was he winding her up in some way?

'Look,' carried on Thornback as if reading her mind, 'this is neither the time nor the place to talk business. Can we meet tomorrow and discuss this further. I'm quite serious, you know.'

That's more like it, thought Angel. 'Okay. If you like I'll meet you for lunch at Greyfish's.'

'Greyfish's at one o'clock. I'll be there.'

Angel turned on her tail and swam back to her

table. Rock was too busy grooving along to Acker Welk to have noticed her absence, she noted.

In fact, she noted wrong. Rock had seen that Thornback had taken an interest in Angel. But he was far too cool to tell Angel that he had noticed. Anyway, Angel was a big girl, quite capable of looking after herself with fish like Thornback. If she was ever in any kind of trouble, the detective knew that it was to him, Rock Salmon, that Angel would turn.

He glanced towards Ray Thornback's table. It was empty. Just then Acker Welk was joined on stage by the eminent Sax player J. Sankworth and the great singer Cleo Ling. The words of the number they chose to sing might have changed the course of Dr Ray Thornback's life had he been there to hear them:

'Don't go swimmin' where ya shouldn't swim, baby. . . .'

3 · Rude Awakening

For several years, Rock Salmon had waged a war of nerves against his alarm clock. The morning after his visit with Angel down to Ronnie Scuba's Dive, he was definitely on the losing side of the war.

It was nine o'clock when the alarm clock decided to spring into action.

'GRRRRRRRRRRRRR!' it said in a loud metallic voice.

This was too much for Rock, who turned over in his bed, and made a weak attempt to knock it off its perch with a rather tired fin. The alarm clock carried on grrrrrr-ing. Rock made another equally weak attempt to counter attack, but failed miserably. The only resort left to him was to pull the pillow over his head.

Sanderson to the rescue. The detective's assistant chose that precise moment to appear with a pot of fresh coffee, which he put down on Rock's desk before turning off the alarm.

'Mmmmm, whazzer time, Sarn'son,' mumbled Rock.

'Time to get up, sir. You're meant to be seeing Professor October at ten o'clock.'

'Professor October?' Rock removed the pillow from his head, and sat up in bed. 'Ouch.'

His head was swimming. It had been a late night.

'You rang me late last night and asked me to fix an urgent appointment with him first thing in the morning, if you remember, sir.'

Slowly the memory of the previous evening came flooding back. Sanderson was right. Professor October, the eminent scientist, was just the guy he needed to see about Dr Ray Thornback. The detective reached for his coffee.

'And what did you get up to last night, Sanderson?'

'Chess, sir. I spent the evening with my friend Gary Caspian trying to crack a rather ingenious variation of the Atlantic Counter Gambit Declined . . .'

'Er, great, Sanderson. We must go through it some time.'

If the truth be known, Rock was rather jealous of Sanderson's prowess on the chess board. Although the detective was more a poker player than a chess expert, he still fancied himself at the game, even if he'd long ago given up trying to beat Sanderson.

'It is a highly interesting piece of conceptual analysis, sir. You see, White's object in the variation is to make space in the centre for . . .'

Rock drifted off back to sleep at this point, only to be woken again by the telephone.

'I'll take that, sir,' said Sanderson. A short pause while the short fish picked up the phone, announced himself and listened. He didn't say a word. After about a minute, he hung up. The expression on his face showed that the phone call had not been pleasant.

Suddenly Rock Salmon was wide awake.

Sanderson swan thoughtfully across the room, wringing his tiny fins.

'Well, Sanderson, who was that?'

'Chief Inspector Hercule Poisson. There's been a murder, sir, as it were.'

'We'd better get on the case, Sanderson.' Rock was up and dressing. 'Who's the victim?'

Sanderson looked the detective straight in the eye. 'Cecil Goldfish, sir.'

'Is that a coincidence or is that a coincidence? Young Sam, my nephew, was with him last night: I saw him alive with my own eyes.'

'Well, "alive" is not how Chief Inspector Poisson just described him, sir. Here's the address. Friend Hercule wants us there right now.'

'Any idea why Poisson wants us?'

'No, sir. He said he'd clue us in when we got there, as it were.'

Rock put on his hat and coat and swam out of the office into the bright waters of 61st Street. Sanderson was on his tail. Rock asked him to get off it.

It was a sunny day. Rock Salmon and Sanderson swam downtown towards Laguna Drive, totally unaware of what was about to happen. . . .

4 · Floating Upwards

Cecil Goldfish had class, whatever that means. To Rock it meant the producer knew how to flaunt his money. To Sanderson it meant he was a frightful snob – as it were.

There was evidence of the movie mogul's wealth long before they actually reached his house. They had to go through security at the small gate-house at the bottom of a long drive. The security guards might well have been relatives of Rock's old friend, Hammerhead. They didn't look like the kind of guys Rock wanted to hang out with.

It took a short while for the heavy mob at Cecil Goldfish's gate-house to clear the two detectives. They spoke through an intercom to the main house, and soon were allowed on their way.

'You know, Sanderson, every time I swim into guys like them I get that same old filleted feeling,' said Rock as they swam towards the main house.

'I know that very feeling, sir. Like they want to take you to the Dry Cleaners.'

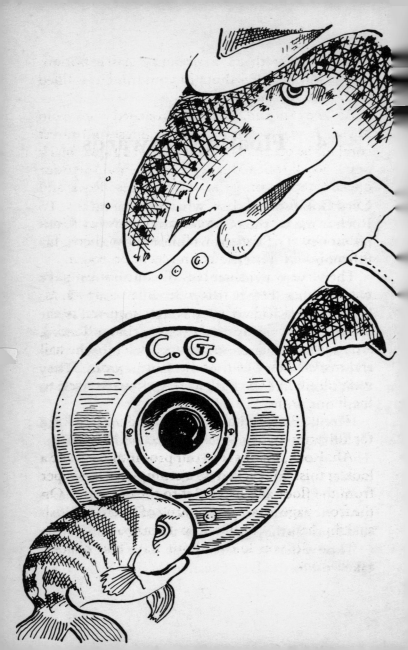

'Ugh, now that's a seriously nasty notion, Sanderson. I always thought your mind was filled with pleasant thoughts.'

As they talked, they approached the main house, It was hewn out of the finest and rarest coral in the ocean. The door bell was a solid black pearl. Rock touched it with his fin and the door opened quietly on its massive hinges. Rock and Sanderson entered.

The two detectives were met by Police Constable Dover, a flatfish well known to them. He ushered them into the main reception room.

The place was a shambles. Goldfish must have put up quite a fight before he floated upwards, thought Rock. There were broken mirrors, ornaments all over the floor, all sorts of things floating around in the water. Rock swam out into the hall and made a quick tour of the other rooms. These were all tidy. The conflict had restricted itself to the living room.

Hercule Poisson had appeared and was looking for fin prints when Rock arrived back there.

'Ah, Rock, thanks for your promptness. Take a look at this.' He picked up a crumpled newspaper from the floor and handed it to the detective. On the front page was a photograph of Cecil Goldfish shaking hands with Dr Ray Thornback.

'What do you know about Ray Thornback?' asked Rock.

37

'Only that he is a scientist who seems to be more interested in self profit than the advance of scientific knowledge. Is there any connection here?'

'I don't know, Inspector,' replied Rock, 'but I intend to find out. Can you leave things to me for a couple of days?'

'Officially, no. But I know your methods, *mon ami*. If you need me, let me know.'

They shook fins and Rock and Sanderson swam back to 61st Street.

An anxious Salmon Davis was waiting for Rock outside his office door.

'Rock, thank cod you're back. I don't know what to do. They want me to leave the day after tomorrow. Contracts haven't been properly sorted out yet. Could be dangerous. Unknown waters. Chance of a lifetime. Can't make up my mind. Not every day a fish like Art Hake rings you up to ask you personally . . .'

'Hey, slow down, Sam. Cool it.' Rock guided his distraught nephew into the office. Sanderson poured some piping wet coffee.

'Here, drink this, sir.'

'Yeah, but waddoIdo? It's a great part in a blockbuster new movie and Ray Thornback is science adviser and I don't trust him after that other thing of his, you know?'

'Hold on, and swallow your bubbles. Okay,

now drink your coffee and let's talk this thing through nice and quietly.'

Sam slurped his coffee. He seemed to relax.

'So, take it from the top, Sam,' said Rock in his most laid-back voice.

'Well, you know how I was approached last night after the theatre to be in an Art Hake movie?'

'Right.'

'After we split up, I swam straight home. There was a note for me. "If you want the part come along to Hollyweed Studios at once."'

'Strange way to do business. Who was the note from?'

'None other than Cecil Goldfish himself,' replied Sam. 'So you see I just had to go along.'

Rock was sure that Sam did not yet know of Cecil Goldfish's demise. He decided not to confuse Sam's account of events with this piece of news.

'With all due respect to you, Sam, you're a mighty small fish in a big pond for a guy like Goldfish to be sending you notes in the middle of the night.'

'I realize that, Rock. That's partly why I swam down to the studio.'

'What happened when you got there?'

'The whole deal was very very fishy: here's what happened . . .'

5 · Fishy Deal

'The waters were real dark. I felt spooked. I got checked through security and swam on to the studio. The place looked deserted. I couldn't see any sign of life. No lights on anywhere. I wasn't sure quite where I was meant to be heading.

'Suddenly, I had company. I froze in my finprints when I got a look at the fish who'd joined me. It was a big shark – and I mean big.

'"Come," he said. I didn't argue. He lead me through the lots to a huge old building. It was real weird swimming through those film sets, I can tell you; following this big shark through an old western town, then a science fiction battleground where they were obviously set up for filming *Starfish Wars*.

'He opened the door and we swam into the past: that's the only way I can describe it. Like the Natural History Museum, know what I mean? Stuffed old fish everywhere, skeletons of prehistoric goofballs. Wow, it was something else, believe me.

'The shark guided me through these strange old dudes until we reached a kind of makeshift office area. A desk was set up. A couple of phones – you get my drift? Seated behind the desk was Art Hake. I recognized him at once, of course.

' "Thanks, The Micky. You can go."

' "Okay, boss."

'Strange name "The Micky", I thought to myself as the big guy swam off out into the night.

' "Yeah, it *is* a strange name," said Art Hake, interrupting my thoughts. "Mako The Micky – Micky The Mako the other way round."

' "Wouldn't catch me taking the micky out of him," I joked.

' "Oh, very drole. Just as well we're not signing you up for your knack at the comedy, Mr Davis."

' "Just what *do* you want me for?" I asked. I had decided to be bold. There was something odd about this meeting.

' "Straight to the point; I like that."

'Art Hake clicked his fins together, rummaged around his desk, and chucked me a script.

' "Check this out."

'I asked if I could take it home. I'm a slow reader. Hake insisted that I read it then and there. He offered me a drink. Looked like it was going to be a late night, judging by the thickness of the script.

'It didn't take me too long to read. It was good stuff. An imaginary expedition through the Straits of Bad Luck to the Precific Ocean, where a huge fish is captured and brought back in captivity. Kind of rang a bell, the story, but I couldn't put it down. I read it from start to fin. Of course, I loved the bits where the monster fell in love with Phay Ray, the heroine.

'My part was the young adventurer who was in love with the heroine, who disapproved of the greedy plans of the wicked explorer in charge of the expedition.

'I loved it, and really wanted the part. Art Hake could see as much by the expression on my face when I'd read the final page.

' "It's yours if you want it. But we leave the day after tomorrow."

' "Where to?"

' "Secret location. Don't want the Press boys blowing the bubbles on it yet."

'He got up from the desk, and swam towards one of the strange prehistoric giants, beckoning me towards him.

' "Listen to me, Sam. Listen well. I am offering you more than just a part in a movie. I am offering you a place in prehistory."

'I couldn't figure the guy out. There was something obsessive about him. But I knew he had me hooked – and he knew that I knew. Just then we were joined by another fish I recognized – Ray Thornback.

'Art Hake introduced us and the scientist announced that he was coming along "for the ride" to the secret location. This was a shot not to be missed, he added.

'To cut a long tale short, Rock, I accepted the part. We all shook fins on it, and I was politely dismissed. Just as I turned to leave, Art Hake told me he would be in contact to tell me where to meet and when.

'I swam through the strange exhibits of giant prehistoric creatures, my heart somewhere between my mouth and my gills. I was excited, but also frightened, if you know what I mean. I also had the feeling that I'd allowed myself to be talked into something that was out of my depth. Everyone knows that guy Ray Thornback is a no-swim area. I decided I needed advice: so here I am, Rock.

'What shall I do?'

6 · Trading Salmons

Rock Salmon and Sanderson listened to Salmon Davis' story with interest.

Rock then told his nephew about the murder of Cecil Goldfish. 'What we don't know yet,' said Sanderson, 'is whether your meeting occured before or after the wicked deed.'

'You mean Thornback and Hake might have had something to do with it?' exclaimed Sam.

'That's what I reckon,' muttered Rock, picking up the phone.

He put a call through to Hercule Poisson, who confirmed that Goldfish had died before the time of Sam Davis' visit to Hollyweed. Rock informed Poisson of his suspicions and he agreed with Rock to hold back so that the detective could get to the bottom of the affair.

'Sam, would you mind not taking part in this film?' asked Rock.

'Of course I would,' said Sam. 'It's my big break.'

'What if I told you that there's a very good chance of you not returning.'

'How do you mean?'

'I mean just that. There's something dirty going on. I reckon that Thornback has done a deal with Art Hake to fund one of his dodgy scientific expeditions.'

'My thought exactly, sir,' continued Sanderson. 'They're not going to any ordinary location to film. Everything points to an expedition to the Precific Ocean.'

'You're pulling my tail,' said Sam. 'There's no proof that such a place exists.'

'Oh, it exists all right,' said Sanderson. 'And I heartily recommend that you don't go there.'

'Well, I don't know. Art Hake's no idiot. He wouldn't be mounting an expensive expedition without a good chance of it succeeding.'

'Yeah', said Rock. 'But he only needs a few feet of real dangerous film to make a fortune. Imagine: TV Special. "Sam Davis meets Monster of the Deep".'

'Okay, okay. I get the picture.'

'So you agree not to go?'

'Okay, Rock. You've talked me out of it.'

'Good. Then I'll go and pretend to be you.'

Sam burst out laughing. 'You can't be serious, Rock. You can't act to save your life.'

'I'm going to have to act to save other fishes'

lives, Sam,' replied the detective gravely. 'Sanderson, get me Professor October on the phone.'

The octopus with whom Rock wanted to get in touch was an old friend. As honest as the day was wet. Professor October was one of the most learned fish of science in the civilized world and would no doubt provide the detective with valuable information about the Precific Ocean.

Rock was therefore disappointed when Sanderson reported that the good Professor was apparently unavailable.

'Oh, well, leave him a message to ring back, Sanderson.'

'I did, sir. Unfortunately, the Professor is going to be out of his lab for some time.'

'Why, where's the sucker going?'

'The Straits of Bad Luck, sir.'

There was a silence in the water. All three fish were thinking much the same thing. Something big was happening, something they did not as yet fully understand, something that had been in the planning stages for some time. Something that had been kept a marine secret from the rest of Atlantis.

The silence was broken by the telephone. Rock answered. Sanderson could tell by the detective's expression that it was Angel Sweetlips. He could also tell that what she said did not please him.

'I absolutely forbid. . . . Okay, I don't have the right to forbid, but you can't, you mustn't, it's. . . . Listen, Angel, please . . . it's too dangerous. . . . Yes, I know you can look after yourself, but. . . . Just don't do it. Don't be a fool. Do you want to wind up high and dry? Hello? Hello?. . . . Oh, Sharks! She's hung up on me.'

Rock put the receiver gently back on its hook, and announced that Angel Sweetlips was on her way to the Straits of Bad Luck.

'What are these Straits of Bad Luck everyone keeps talking about?' asked Sam.

'According to Sir Isaac Newt, they're the entrance to the Precific Ocean,' said Sanderson, slowly.

'Listen, I'd better go back to your place, Sam. You stay here with Sanderson. From now until I get back, you're Rock Salmon.'

'Great, does that mean I get to go down to Ronnie Scuba's Dive every night?'

'Sanderson, look after him. Make sure he behaves himself.'

'I really think I ought to come with you, sir, as it were.'

'Somebody's got to mind the shop, Sanderson. What if a case comes up?'

'You think I can't handle it, Rock?' asked Sam.

'Wise guy, huh?' replied the detective, with a smile. 'Sanderson, you've got a full-time job on your fins. Good luck.'

'Same to you, sir,' replied the tiny fish.

Good luck was what Rock needed, he felt, as he swam out of the office up town towards his nephew's pad. He had no doubt that within a very short while he'd be on his way to the Straits of Bad Luck, and from there into the Precific Ocean.

There had been many moments in Rock's life when the immediate future looked far from clear. This was one of them. All that was clear to Rock was that his future lay in the past. . . .

7 · Profish

It was hot stormy prehistoric weather. Inimus found it hard to breathe. His gills felt clogged up, and he was in a mild state of misery. The only good thing about his present condition was that he couldn't smell DinoCod who, much as Inimus was fond of him, really was a swimming disaster area smell-wise.

Inimus and DinoCod were making the most of the hot stormy weather. They'd decided to spend the day taking fire lessons with old Profish.

This strange fish was another outsider in the prehistoric fish community. He was scaly, bony and ugly all at once. His mouth was too big for his body, and he had the most hideous 'thing' stuck on the side of his face. This 'thing' looked like a cross between a television aerial and a piece of extended bubble gum.

Profish was considered to be a harmless old eccentric by most. He claimed to be able to see into the time to come, and for many years now

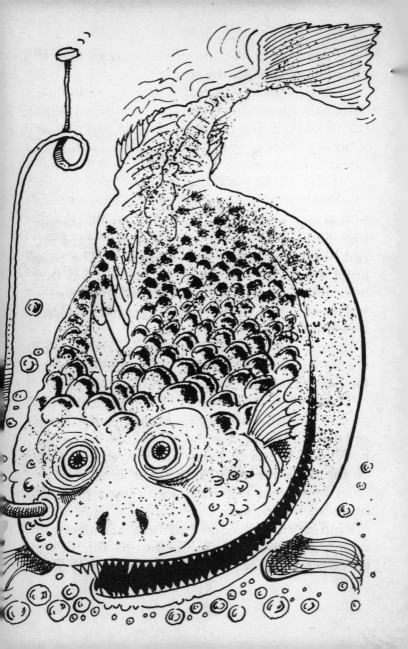

had warned of the day when strange tiny fish would come from the future.

He had also once had a strange vision of a scientific revolution; gill–less creatures rubbing what looked like two bits of coral together and causing flames. FIRE. Ever since, Profish had held fire lessons.

It has to be said that no one took Profish seriously. But he was a gentle soul, who wouldn't harm an amoeba, so everyone in the Precific Ocean left him to his dreams and visions in peace.

Inimus was very fond of Profish, despite the fact that he never understood a word he said. As he and DinoCod squatted outside the old fish's cave rubbing coral, he felt wet, tranquil and contented.

'You know, everyone thinks you're daft, Profish. You have to admit, you are a bit weird.'

'Searun past Eve and Adam round swerve of beach and bend of cod past health centre and environs leading to a load of old fishwives,' replied Profish.

Inimus shook his head. He hadn't understood a word, but there was no mistaking the look on Profish's face. He was happy to have company.

'Don't seem to be having much luck with this fire, Profish,' muttered DinoCod.

'In the fin is my beginning,' replied Profish, nodding his ugly head sagely and twitching his

TV aerial. DinoCod's aroma taxed even the most caring and benign fish.

'You mean we have to keep on trying,' suggested Inimus.

'What a piece of work is fish, how noble in reason,' suggested Profish, rubbing away at his coral with a glazed gaze.

'I don't know why we do this stuff,' complained DinoCod to Inimus. 'It doesn't work, and old Profish is as batty as a fishcake.'

'It just feels good,' replied Inimus. 'I don't know why; it makes no sense to me either. Look at him.' Both of them stared at Profish and burst out laughing. Profish, far from being offended, joined their laughter.

Suddenly, there was an almighty roar. Profish screamed, and urged his two young friends inside his cave. Inimus and DinoCod didn't need urging. They both knew the fearsome call of Greatwhiteosaurus Rex – undisputed boss of the Precific Ocean. It was G.R.'s lunchtime, and he was a legend in his own lunchtime.

'Life is so primitive,' mumbled Profish.

8 · The Straits

Sure enough, the expected call for Salmon Davis came from the studio the following evening. Rock Salmon was sitting in his nephew's jaccuzzi, reading gossip stories about the great Hollyweed stars, when the visitor arrived.

'Why, top of the evening to you, The Micky,' said Rock airily. From his nephew's description there could be no doubt that the visitor was indeed the overgrown Mako Shark.

The Micky grunted and told Rock to follow him. So far so good, thought Rock. He thinks I'm Salmon Davis. And why not? When you've seen one Dogfish, you've seen them all.

There was only one fish on the expedition who would know he wasn't Sam – Angel Sweetlips. It was vital he speak to her to prevent her being alarmed and giving the game away.

After a long swim to the dreary backwaters of Atlantis, Rock, alias Sam, finally met up with some of his fellow travellers. He didn't know any of the other three fish in his party.

One was an old looking fish who introduced himself to Rock as a journalist called Colefish. Another was a rather tough looking nurse shark called Nurse Iceberg. The third was an interesting fish – apparently an archaeologist who'd forgotten his name.

'What do you mean, you've forgotten your name?' Rock asked as the small expedition swam towards the small local seatrain station.

'Why, there are far more important things for me to store in my head than my name.'

'Well, well, well,' commented Colefish. 'Haven't heard anything like that since the year Bluegill won the silver single-handed in the Ironian Mixed Doubles.'

It's going to be a long hard journey, thought Rock. I hope they're not all mad as monkfish.

It took two days to reach the Straits of Bad Luck. Two days of changing seatrains, swimming through dangerous reefs and currents, snatching sleep whenever they could.

When they arrived, they were amazed to find that there was a small town right at the entrance. The town was reached via a narrow channel of water – single-line swimming only.

There was a large sign at the perimeter which read:

WELCOME TO DICE CITY.
YOU NEVER KNOW YOUR LUCK.

Dice City wasn't a city at all. It looked like something in the Hollyweed Studio – a perfect replica of an old western cowboy town.

Naturally, they all headed for the local saloon, which was also the hotel. And it was there that they met up with the other main members of the expedition – Art Hake, Ray Thornback, and Professor October.

Rock was not at all surprised to see the old octopus. It made sense for this eminent scientist to be on the expedition. Rock was sure that he had had nothing to do with Cecil Goldfish's murder. He probably didn't know anything about it. Just who *did* know about it, Rock was anxious to find out. But he had to be patient, or else he'd completely blow his cover.

Where was Angel Sweetlips? Rock had to get to her before she spotted him in the party. This question at least was answered quickly.

The party of fish were all summoned by Mako The Micky to assemble for a briefing by Ray Thornback. It was here that Rock spotted Angel. Before he could attract her attention, however, Thornback started to speak.

'Okay, now I'm not too good at words. I just want to tell you that I'm glad you could all make

57

it. It's going to be worth your while. Tomorrow morning we head off through the Straits of Bad Luck into waters unknown. Thanks to Art Hake here and Cecil Goldfish, who financed the expedition, we're taking a specialist film crew with us and two actors, Salmon Davis and Angel Sweetlips.'

Thornback pointed helpfully at Rock and Angel. Fortunately Angel was too far away from Rock to notice he was Rock.

'Only thing I want to say,' continued Thornback, 'is stick together, don't try to get smart, and any problems, come to me: I'll do what I can to help. Oh, yes. We're going to come up against some fairly weird creatures. On no account is anyone to harm them. We are here to further our knowledge of our planet so that we can improve life below water. Thank you.'

Rock found it hard to think that the speaker of these words was a bad guy. But you can't judge an oyster by its shell. After his talk, Thornback invited Rock to meet Angel.

'Angel Sweetlips, have you met Salmon Davis? He was rather good in the musical "My Fair Fish". I believe it cost Sam Goldfish a small fortune to buy him out of his contract.'

Angel looked at Rock, and said, 'Pleased to meet you Mr Davis. Actually, we have met before. Aren't you the nephew of Rock Salmon, the detective? There is a resemblance. Of course, Rock looks much older than you. . . .'

'Ms Sweetlips, how nice to see you again. I look forward to working with you. Uncle Rock? He's not that old you know. Looks rather fit for one of his years.'

They smiled at one another. There was no doubt in Rock's mind that Angel knew who he was, but she'd realized he was not simply along here pretending to be Sam for a joyride.

'Looking forward to working with you, Sam. Now if you'll excuse me, I think I'm going to get some sleep. It's going to be a long day tomorrow.'

They all said good-night. It wasn't long before Rock himself decided to turn in. He had a dreamless night's sleep.

The following morning, they were all up bright and early. It was a beautiful wet day as the expedition set off into the Straits of Bad Luck.

The Straits were so narrow that they virtually had to swim through in single file. They consisted of sheer cliffs of dark rough rock which seemed to hang gauntly from the surface to the depths of the dark grey sea.

The swim was not easy. Strange currents seemed to drag them back, as if warning them not to go on. The currents would change without warning and pull them through at an alarming speed. And then the other currents would take over

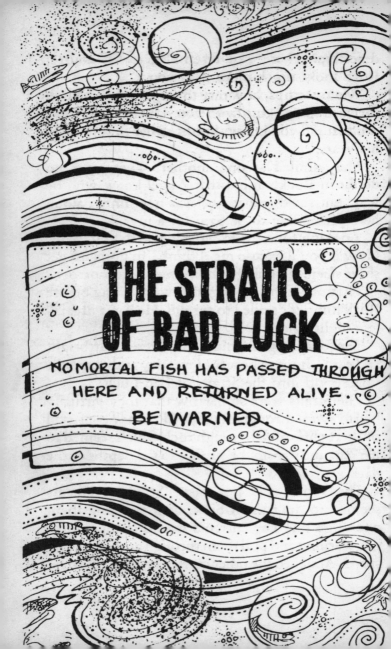

once again – a continual process of yes and no, stop and go, swim on, swim back.

Then they came across the sign. Rock had not been prepared for this. It was an almighty great billboard with a daunting message:

THE STRAITS OF BAD LUCK:
NO MORTAL FISH HAS PASSED
THROUGH HERE
AND RETURNED ALIVE. BE WARNED.

Everyone pretended to ignore this unignorable warning. Everyone was feeling brave – for the time being.

It took them about three hours to swim through the Straits of Bad Luck. None of them was quite sure what to expect at the other end. Had they reached the Precific Ocean? If they had, why did the waters feel exactly the same? Where were all the monsters of the deep?

Little did they know that at that very moment the strange and ugly prehistoric Profish was whispering, 'soon, strange creatures of the future, soon!'

9 · **Monstrous Pastimes**

Inimus and DinoCod came out of Profish's cave into the sunlight. Profish himself was garbling gobbledegook they couldn't understand: stuff about the future, or so DinoCod reckoned.

Profish was saying things like: 'Microchip quarter pounder back to the future finflopping through punk video swim time. . . .'

'Better leave him to it, I reckon,' muttered Inimus.

So off they swam to find somewhere else to do their own swim. They decided to head towards the Deep Pit.

Often frequented by the younger Precifics, the Deep Pit was great fun. Here the waters were so deep that you could drop a shell and not hear it reach the bottom for three weeks.

There was also a major chance of spotting some of the really weird deep sea fish who were known to hang out there. But this would be an added bonus. The main attraction for both Inimus and

DinoCod was that the Deep Pit was quiet. None of the other monsters of the deep bothered to go there. And both Inimus and DinoCod were habitually made fun of by fish their own age, so they tended not to mix.

They had to swim past lived-in caves to reach the Deep Pit, and this meant running the gauntlet of bullies of their own age. Too bad. They managed to get by with only a couple of jibes of 'Hey, short pants,' and 'Yugh, hold your nose, folks,' and soon reached their destination.

They suspended themselves near the surface of the deep pit, idly flapping their tails in the still, sombre waters. Neither of them said a word. They were both intent on trying to spot a monster or denizen that was even more monstrous and denizenish than either of them.

At first, they had no luck: nothing but nothing. After a while Inimus saw movement. It was nothing much, just a small flurry deep deep down, such a small flurry that DinoCod missed it. They both stared, waiting to see if it would come to anything. Nothing.

'Must have imagined it,' muttered Inimus.

They sat there in the water for a while before they both saw the flurry.

'There, there: I told you,' exclaimed Inimus.

'Yes, I see it too,' agreed DinoCod.

What was a flurry suddenly reared up fast from

the depths towards the two fish and became a large cavernous set of very nasty teeth, teeth that were heading straight towards them.

'Swim for it, DinoCod,' yelled Inimus.

They took off as fast as they could, just in the nick of time. The set of nasty teeth snapped at where they'd been sitting, narrowly missing them both. Behind the teeth were ten metres of monstrosity.

The two fish swam for all they were worth towards the caves where they lived, scared out of their bubbles.

They reached The Great Regnoc's cave and were for once delighted to see his dreadfully bad paintings. They, at least, were familiar and gave them a warm secure feeling.

Meanwhile, the expedition from Atlantis was still wondering when they would reach the Precific Ocean. They'd stopped at the furthest end of the Straits of Bad Luck where the narrow channel widened into open barren waters.

'According to my charts, we get taken by current through the Sea of Anger,' muttered Thornback.

He was right. He was still in mid-mutter when the entire party was dragged downwards. It was like being sucked down the plughole of a gigantic bath. There were screams and shouts from all of them. Rock Salmon's first thought was for the safety of Angel Sweetlips, but there was absolutely nothing he could do except trust himself to the pressure that was sucking him down through the water.

Down they plunged until finally they arrived in the most agitated angry waters they had ever encountered: the Sea of Anger.

At least they all seemed to have arrived together. Art Hake counted heads. Yes, all present. Rock took the opportunity to swim up beside Angel.

'Isn't this fun?' she exclaimed.

'Fun? You must be joking. It's not my idea of fun. I'd rather be back home in Atlantis. I'd even rather be sitting through some dried up musical than be here. And it's not going to get better, you can bet on that.'

'Where's your sense of adventure, Rock, er, I mean Sam?'

Luckily no one seemed to have overheard Angel's slip of the lip. They were too busy flapping their gills, trying to keep their balance in the angry seas.

What's next? wondered the detective. Professor October knew the answer. According to Lewis MacCarol, after the Sea of Anger came the Waters of Syrup.

Sure enough, the expedition soon found itself

up to the gills in sticky waters so thick and gooey that they were unable to flap their tails. The only movement came from the natural flow of the water. The whole effect of the Waters of Syrup was to make them feel they were suspended in some strange time warp, a sort of elevator, going down, back into the past.

They all knew to a fish they were well and truly on their way to the Precific Ocean.

There was no sense in fighting the Waters of Syrup. Rock actually found the whole experience quite relaxing. It was like being wrapped up in seaweed, being gently wafted back through time. He felt his eyes grow sleepy. He started to drift off, as did all the members of the expedition.

None of them were to see the true beginning of the Precific Ocean. Within a very short time, they arrived.

10 · Little and Large

Inimus soon got bored hanging around the cave with The Great Regnoc, who was not a great talker. DinoCod had long since gone home, kicked out by the painter because of his vile aroma.

Inimus felt lonely. There was nothing at all for him to do, no one for him to swim out with. He decided to go back to the Deep Pit. At least that had been exciting, and he was sure the danger had now passed.

It didn't take him long to get there and he was surprised to find he was not alone. There, floating at the edge, was Profish, the strange prophet. He was performing a strange tribal ritual, rubbing the inevitable sticks of coral together, and dancing a very odd dance.

'What are you doing, Profish?'

'Hush, Inimus. This is where it will arrive.'

'What, you mean the big guy with the crazy teeth?'

'This is where the future will arrive.'

'No. This guy was very much the present. Must be someone different you're expecting.'

Inimus sat and watched Profish performing his ritual. He felt very sorry for him. Why did he behave so oddly?

Meanwhile the expedition from Atlantis had definitely arrived in the Precific Ocean – and they knew it. While Inimus and Profish were sitting at the top of the Deep Pit, somehow Ray Thornback and Co. were at the bottom. Much was to happen before they confronted each other.

The bottom of the Deep Pit was unbearably dark. Fortunately, the expedition had come prepared for this. Torch lights were used to illumine the darkness. Much good they did. There was little to see, only rocks and sand – like any other deserted sea bed.

They soon learned that this was no ordinary sea bed. Mako The Micky was nosing around the ocean floor, when he got a nasty shock. Something grabbed his snout, something so big that he jumped back in horror and fear. The disturbed sand created a blinding cloud in the water. For a while, no one could see a thing. When the cloud settled, they were face to face with a fish that was at least ten times the size of Mako The Micky.

The big fish must have had as big a surprise as The Micky. It had never seen such a tiny crowd of fish. A signal was sent from its stomach to its brain that dinner time had arrived, and the giant sprang into action.

Fortunately for the expedition and particularly Mako The Micky, it was quite a long distance from stomach to brain in the giant fish, so they were able to scatter for their lives, and hide behind rocks.

There was nothing the big fish could do. He tried digging them out, but to no avail. He decided to look for lunch elsewhere. Hiding behind his rock with Angel Sweetlips, Rock Salmon had time to reflect. Here he was on a frighteningly dangerous mission, trying to find out whether Art Hake and Ray Thornback had anything to do with the murder of Sam Goldfish. There must be easier ways to make a living, he thought.

He wondered what Sanderson and Salmon Davis were up to at that moment, back home in the modern comfort of Atlantis. Probably watching TV with a take-away prawnburger, he chuckled.

He didn't chuckle for long. He was suddenly and violently pushed down by Angel.

'Look out!' she screamed.

Rock looked up. He was staring into the giant eyes of a very giant squid. Moreover, the rocks behind which he and Angel and the rest of the expedition were hiding had started to move. They weren't rocks at all. They were the huge tentacles of the squid.

'Holy Fish,' exclaimed Rock. 'We're sunk.'

Slowly the tentacles started to contract and turn inwards. There was no time for them to do anything. They were completely powerless. The tentacles, each with a hundred giant suckers on them, began to squeeze. Even Professor October was victim to them, despite being a distant if minuscule relation.

They seemed to be drawn inwards towards the beast's cavernous mouth. Rock drew Angel towards him to shut out the sight of what was about to happen. Somewhere in the distance, the detective saw a blinding light, a shaft of sunlight. So this is what it's like to die, thought Rock. He had been close to death many times before, but had never experienced its closeness in such technicolour slow-motion.

Suddenly, all pressure stopped. The giant giant squid had released them, flinging them all into even deeper water. Rock was vaguely aware of the giant monster heading towards the blinding light.

They headed quickly for what turned out to be real rocks. They all looked up to see what was happening. The squid was swimming fast towards the surface. What had caused the blinding light? Was it simply sunlight? Not possible. So, if not, who had saved them?

This was a question that would have to be answered later. The incident with the squid had attracted the attention of other creatures of the Precific Ocean.

Slowly, gradually, Rock was aware of strange eyes appearing from the gloom on all sides. He had the horrible feeling that a lobster must have when it has been captured by man and put in a tank ready to be cooked alive.

Rock counted seven eyes. A peculiar number, he noted. Indeed three monsters had spotted him and his group. Two icthyosaurs made straight for the rocks and effortlessly prised out two unfortunate camera operators and their equipment. They quickly munched through these, accompanied by ghoulish screams. The water became clouded with blood. Angel buried her head in Rock's shoulder.

The third set of eyes turned towards the two icthyosaurs. It was Greatwhiteosaurus Rex. And he was angry. He viewed this part of the ocean as his own private dining room. What right had these two clumsy old fish to steal his horsd'oeuvre?

Realizing what was about to happen, one icthyosaur turned towards the other and said, 'Oh, oh – trouble!'

G. Rex turned towards them and roared. The two monsters had a decision to make: swim for it,

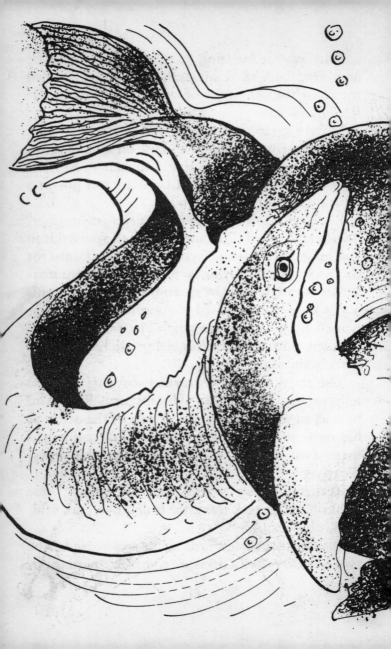

or fight. Sadly, these creatures were not very good at making quick decisions. Their minds were made up for them. G. Rex attacked, making a full frontal charge. The force of his impact sent all three monsters flying. They twisted and flayed, churning up the water like a primaeval washing machine.

For a while, G. Rex looked as if he was gaining the upper fin. The surprise factor was on his side. But the two icthyosaurs gradually organized themselves, realizing that there were two of them and only one of their foe.

Rock Salmon was spellbound. He had seen Great White Sharks fighting in the waters around Big Reef. They were big enough for him. But these creatures were ten times the size. It was like watching three cartoon office blocks fighting – and fighting to the death.

There was blood everywhere. Icth 1 tore into G. Rex's tail, while Icth 2 grabbed his dorsal fin. G. Rex in the meantime twisted and turned, gnashing his jagged teeth, trying to connect with flesh, to no avail. There was no doubt he was beginning to weaken. His two foes noticed this, and one of them slackened his attack for a moment. Mistake. G. Rex sensed the pace slackening, and mustered up all his strength.

With a giant wrench, he turned and grabbed Icth 2 by the throat, and took one deep fatal bite.

Icth 1 realized too late what was happening. He didn't know what to do. Once again, his slow brain let him down. And it was all over. Greatwhiteosaurus Rex turned towards him, letting Icth 2 go to float upwards, and then charged. Five minutes later, G. Rex was free to set to work on his lunch: 'Atlantis Expedition on the Rocks'.

But the expedition, motivated by Dr Ray Thornback, had swum for it.

Rock, in his relief, forgot all about the seventh eye. What had that been?

11 · Timetrap

The expedition had managed to find an apparently empty cave. Here Ray Thornback held a frantic briefing session.

'It's too dangerous for us here. We've already lost our cameras, so we can't film. If only we could capture just one specimen. . . .'

'Don't be crazy. What chance would we have of that?' exclaimed Art Hake.

'You're quite right,' agreed Thornback. 'We've already lost two lives. I don't want to be responsible for any more accidents.'

Rock was pleasantly surprised to hear these words. Perhaps Ray Thornback had not been involved with the murder of Cecil Goldfish after all. Either that or he was a good actor.

'Don't forget one thing!' It was Professor October's turn to make a point. 'No fish has ever returned to civilization from the Precific Ocean.'

'At least, not back through the Straits of Bad Luck,' agreed Thornback.

'You mean there's another route?'

'We'll swim under that bridge when we get to it,' said Thornback. 'Meanwhile, how do we get out of here without being eaten?'

Inimus was feeling very lonely. Nobody wanted to have anything to do with him. He hated being so little. He wanted to feel big. There had been some action somewhere deep down within the Deep Pit, but it had been too far down for him to see. He'd thought he'd spotted a couple of dead Icthyosaurs floating upwards, but he may have been mistaken.

His spirits were low as he swam towards the deserted cave where he often spent time alone. He was about to swim in when he heard voices. How amazing; in all the years he'd been swimming to this cave, he had never met another creature, not even his friend DinoCod. He hid at the entrance and peered inside.

Sure enough, there were fish talking. He'd never seen fish so tiny – far smaller than him. They were talking about trying to escape back to their home waters.

'Er, maybe I can help,' he said in his gentlest, most quiet voice.

The reaction to his words was most unexpected. The tiny fish all leapt for cover.

'No, it's all right. I won't hurt you,' said Inimus. 'Tell me, where you come from are all the

77

creatures small like you?'

Ray Thornback thought it his moral duty to stand out and address this strange but friendly monster. All the rest of the expedition were hiding in the corners of the cave – including Rock Salmon.

Dr Thornback swam boldly out from behind a rock and looked up at the giant conger eel that was Inimus.

'Who are you?' asked Thornback, in his deepest voice.

'My name's Cong, but everyone round here calls me Inimus because I'm so small.'

The entire expedition relaxed. They came out from their various corners to hear the exchange between Inimus and Thornback.

'To us you're a giant, Cong.'

'I gather. That's terrific. I mean – it makes a change. Listen, this may sound odd but can I come and visit your part of the ocean? I hate it here. Nobody takes me seriously because I'm so little.'

'Of course you can come and visit, Cong. You can come back with us right now, if you'd like to.'

'Really? Oh, that would be great.'

'No it wouldn't,' exclaimed Angel.

Inimus looked upset. Thornback quickly interrupted her. 'Shut up, you. Can't you see this is our big chance? We'll make a fortune.'

'Listen, Cong. If you come back to Atlantis with us, you'll get treated like some giant freak. You wouldn't like that, would you?'

Cong looked at Angel, and then at Thornback.

'Everyone treats me like a freak here anyway. I think I'd rather be a big freak than a little one for a change. Thanks for the warning though, Miss.'

'Okay then, that's settled. You can come back with us.'

Colefish was absolutely delighted. 'Well, well, well,' he exclaimed. 'I haven't seen the like of this since well before I was born.'

'That's all very well,' muttered Art Hake. 'But how do we get out of here and back to Atlantis?'

'Through the Timetrap,' announced Profish.

Everyone turned towards the mouth of the cave. They hadn't realized there was another monster in their presence. They all hid again in their various hiding places.

'Oh, don't be frightened,' said Inimus, soothingly. 'It's only Profish.'

'What's this about a Timetrap?' asked Thornback.

'Through the back of the cave to the world beyond where the grey grey sea murmurs on and on of a future sea where life is free and everyone can watch TV,' announced Profish, pointing at the dark recesses at the back of the cave.

'Simple as that, eh?' asked Rock.

'Let's give it a whirl then,' suggested Professor October, propelling himself inkily towards the rear of the cave.

12 · Meanwhile...

Life in Atlantis went on as normal – well, almost as normal. In order to suppress rumours, Hercule Poisson had leaked it to the Press that Cecil Goldfish had joined Art Hake and Co. on a major film shoot in distant seas.

Rock's office on West 61st Street was a mess. Sanderson had announced he was going to follow up a lead on the case out of town, and Salmon Davis was treating the place as his own: parties every night, loud music. Fortunately, it was located in the business quarter of town. Most of the other offices were not inhabited at night.

Salmon Davis' routine was simple. Down to Ronnie Scuba's Dive, then back to Rock's office around midnight. Fish were beginning to talk. What had got into Rock Salmon?

Ronnie Scuba himself noticed the change. Rock was an old friend, and the club owner noticed that he seemed to have drastically changed his living habits. The old crooner put this down to the fact that Angel Sweetlips had apparently left town with Art Hake. No wonder Rock was depressed.

One morning, Sam opened his bleary eyes, swam over some sleeping friends on the floor after last night's routine party, poured some coffee, and glanced at the newspaper.

He was horrified to see an article about his Uncle Rock. Apparently, he'd raised whoopee the night before down at the Hippodrown, and ended up being thrown out on his gill.

'Tut, tut, Uncle Rock. You bad fish.' It was only after a cup of strong coffee and some reflection that he realized that it was *him* the article was about, not his Uncle Rock.

'Hey, maybe I should dry it up a bit. Uncle Rock's not going to be too happy when he comes home – if he comes home.'

Sam was genuinely fond of his uncle, and he started clearing up the apartment, as if that would balance out his guilty feelings for managing to launch Rock Salmon's name into the gossip columns.

As he did so, there was a ring on the door and in swam Hercule Poisson unannounced. The police chief smiled wryly as he scanned his eye round the office. There were bodies everywhere, sleeping in what looked like the most uncomfortable positions. There was even one goggle-eyed fish sleeping on the ceiling.

'While the dogfish is away, eh, mon ami?'

'Yeah. Hold on, I'm a dogfish too, you know.'

'You could have fooled me. Anyway, I have some news. They're on their way back. They arrived at Sea Freeze late last night.'

'Hey, how about that?'

'Which means you've got approximately twenty-four hours to clean up this office. Where's Sanderson?'

'Oh, he hasn't been around for ages. Said he was following up a lead on the Goldfish murder. Hey, Inspector, thanks for telling me Uncle Rock's on his way back. I appreciate it.'

'Just clean the place up, eh?'

Poisson left, and Sam woke up all his sleeping friends. 'Party's over everyone; time to go home now.'

Hercule Poisson was puzzled, although he hadn't admitted so to Salmon Davis. What was Sanderson up to? The Chief Inspector had long ago come to the conclusion that Ray Thornback and Art Hake were the only two fish who might have killed Cecil Goldfish. Despite his continued, if discreet, investigations while Rock was away, he had discovered no further evidence of anyone else being involved.

So why should Sanderson be out of town following leads? It was a mystery.

He was so deep in thought that he didn't see the

headlines on all the latest editions on the news stands as he swam past:

RAY THORNBACK CAPTURES
MONSTER OF THE DEEP:
KING CONGER IS COMING
TO ATLANTIS!

13 · Brave New World

'Listen, Cong. We're going to have to think this thing through carefully. I mean, we'll have to pretend you're a prisoner, okay?'

'Why, Doctor Thornback?'

'Well, it just won't do to have you swimming around, enjoying yourself, that's all. Not in the beginning, at any rate. We'll have to let the fish back home in Atlantis get used to you. Don't forget, you're going to scare the scales off them.'

'Who, me? Really?'

Inimus was thrilled. What a difference being feared. The gullible monster was willing to agree to anything.

'Well, I think it's disgusting and degrading,' announced Angel Sweetlips.

'Yeah, me too,' said Rock.

Art Hake and Ray Thornback weren't having anything of it. They recognized that Inimus was a once in a fishtime opportunity to wash up the bucks, and no one was going to stop them.

'What's the harm, anyway? It was Cong's idea in the first place.'

Rock and Angel couldn't disagree. They were both tired. All they wanted to do was get home to Atlantis. It had been a long, boring and uneventful journey through the Timetrap to Sea Freeze.

Rock was confused. He had swum along on the expedition to try to catch a murderer. Like Hercule Poisson, he had been convinced that Art Hake or Ray Thornback were behind the death of Cecil Goldfish. The problem was that throughout the duration of the expedition, Ray Thornback had behaved like a good and indeed brave fish, who had taken a very responsible attitude to his job.

Similarly, Art Hake had shown both enterprise and courage on the trip. True, they were now both intent on exploiting Inimus, on turning him into King Conger. But Inimus really *was* King Conger, so where was the real harm in that?

But if Hake and Thornback were not the murderers, then who was? Mako The Micky had turned out to be a rather gentle shark after all. And he would do nothing unless at the order of his boss.

Perhaps Sanderson would have some ideas.

'No, sir. I'm as puzzled as you are, as it were.'

Rock was delighted to be back home in Atlantis. He had decided not to enter the city with the others. He couldn't bear the idea of all the publicity. Art Hake had had a special 'cage' designed for Inimus. For the grand entrance into Atlantis Inimus, of course, was not on view. First sight of him would be before a paying audience, with bucks changing fins to secure TV and video rights, etc, etc. . . .

Sanderson was playing chess with his computer when Rock arrived back. The detective was thrilled to see his tiny assistant.

'Oh, Sanderson, you would have hated it. Giant fish – I can't possibly describe them to you. Ten times as big as a Great White Shark. Can you imagine? Of course there were quite a few bad scenes, I can tell you; but we all pulled through.'

'I know, sir. I was with you all the way.'

'That's a comforting thought, Sanderson.'

'No, sir. I can tell you now. I was with you all the way. Remember the beam of light when the giant squid was about to eat you? That was me. Remember the seven eyes?'

'You mean you were with us all the way?'

'Yes, sir. That's what I just said, as it were. And I know who Cecil Goldfish's murderer is.'

'Tell me, Sanderson. Tell me.'

'Sir, I'd love to, as it were. But it's important that just for a little while you don't know. You see, I still need concrete proof.'

'Well, I don't know why you can't tell me,

87

Sanderson.' Rock was offended.

'I know how you feel. But please trust me, sir. I've told Inspector Poisson, and he's agreed to go along with my plan.'

The news that Sanderson had been on the trip the whole time bewildered Rock. The logic behind Sanderson's secrecy did not. It was a very clever idea, thoroughly in keeping with Sanderson, whose middle name, after all, was 'Camouflage'.

Rock phoned his nephew to thank him for being him in his absence.

'No problem, Uncle Rock. Any time. How did you enjoy being me?'

'It was real easy, Sam. I just swam along and tried to look stupid all day.'

Sam laughed. The tone in his uncle's voice was friendly. He obviously hadn't read any back issues of the gossip papers yet.

'You can't have found that too hard, Rock. Say, was I good in the movie?'

'There was no movie, Sam.'

Rock gave Sam a potted shrimp version of his adventure.

'... Anyway,' he concluded, 'you have the chance to meet King Conger on the weekend. He's appearing in a mega spectacular at the Atlantis Bowl.'

'Great. Can you get me some tickets?'

'That's the least I can do. They'll be with you tomorrow.'

They said goodbye and hung up.

Inimus was very excited. The whole thing had been like a dream. He had agreed to perform in Dr Thornback's circus routine. It was the only way, apparently, that he would be accepted in this future world.

When he arrived in Atlantis, he was stunned by the way civilization had progressed. It seemed that the fish had somehow shrunk, while their dwellings had grown. How extraordinary. And there were so many fish. Although he was in a 'cage', which was covered up for the journey, he was able to watch the outside world on something called closed circuit TV.

He had everything he needed inside his cage. And he knew that he was a celebrity. If only DinoCod could see him now. How proud he'd be. Profish had been right. Oh brave new world that has such sea fish in it.

Inimus was really looking forward to his stage debut. He had agreed to stay 'under wraps' until the weekend, in order to gain maximum impact with the punters. He was really looking forward to pretending to be a monster. He hadn't been sure about that at first, but Ray Thornback had persuaded him that a certain amount of 'showbiz hype' was essential.

'It's all good clean wet fun,' added Thornback.

Inimus, alias King Conger, was very fond of Ray Thornback. But he did not like Art Hake. Here was a fish that for some reason he did not trust. There was something dry in his manner. And this smooth dry film director seemed to have some kind of hold over Thornback. Inimus may have been prehistoric, but he wasn't stupid. He noticed these things. Of all the fish he had met, his favourite was Angel Sweetlips. He loved the way she hated the idea of him being a circus performer. Her fears were totally foolish, of course. He was quite capable of looking after himself. After all, he was King Conger. He was a monster of the deep. If he didn't like his situation, he could swim off at any time. That was what had been agreed.

He was looking forward to seeing Angel Sweetlips at his debut. She had promised him she'd be there.

14 · King Conger

The great day had come. Atlantis was bursting at the seams with weekend visitors anxious to be among the first to see King Conger. There had not been much time to organize the Press, but Art Hake's Hollyweed machine had gone into action. All the media were primed to cover the big event.

The Atlantis Bowl was packed full as a mega-sardine tin hours before the show was due to begin. Backstage was a dive of activity. The Starfish Girls, who were to open the show, were busy rehearsing. Salmon Davis (the real one) and Ethel Mermaid were practising a song specially and hastily written for the occasion by Ike and Tina Tuna.

Inimus was left to himself in his giant cage. He was in a state of anticlimax. Now that his debut was about to happen, he had gone off the idea. What was it all about, this showbiz hype? Nothing much he could do now. He'd agreed to go along with all the arrangements. He wished Angel

Sweetlips was with him. She had warned him.

Rock Salmon knew that King Conger's debut was his last big chance to solve the mystery of Cecil Goldfish's murder. All the main characters in the drama would be assembled in the celebrity enclosure of the Atlantis Bowl. Hercule Poisson was primed and ready to close in at the appropriate moment. What did Sanderson know that he didn't, Rock wondered.

At eight o'clock precisely, the Atlantis Phinharmonic Orchestra started playing, and the lights went down. On swam the Starfish Sisters. Sanderson was in the celebrity enclosure with Art Hake, Angel Sweetlips, Mako The Micky, Professor October, Colefish, Nurse Iceberg and an archaeologist who'd forgotten his name. Rock Salmon was backstage with Ray Thornback. The detective was dressed up in the same clothes as his nephew. Obviously there was no way he could pretend to rehearse with a pro like Ethel Mermaid, so this was the best they could think of to allow him to snoop without being detected.

The Starfish Sisters were a great hit as usual. Halfway through their number, King Conger's covered cage was moved on stage. This caused the crowd to gasp. The whole thing was being brilliantly stage-managed to gain maximum dramatic effect.

On swam Ethel Mermaid and Salmon Davis,

singing the 'King Conger' Song. This was scored to build up to a huge chorus, and when the two singers reached the punch lines –

'If you thought the sea had seven wonders,
You couldn't have been wronger.
You don't have to wait; here's number eight –
The greatest of them all – KING CONGER . . .'

The orchestra played a crashing chord, Sam and Ethel swam off, and the lights went down. A single spotlight focused on a position just in front of King Conger's cage.

Inside, Inimus was petrified. He'd lost all his confidence. He felt like a fraud. He wanted to go home. Too late. On swam Ray Thornback into the spotlight. Ominous pulsating drums began to play in a primaeval rhythm. And Ray Thornback started to tell the story of King Conger.

It was a theatrical account, with all the right amount of exaggeration; tales of courage, of adventure, of bravery in the face of grave danger. Stories about giant monsters of the deep, but none of them more giant than the creature they saw before them, who had put up a fierce struggle but finally succumbed. KING CONGER.

Angel Sweetlips squirmed in embarassment and disgust. Art Hake was up out of his seat in anger.

'Hey, that son of a fishmonger's changed the

script. We promised Inimus we were going to let everyone know he was friendly.'

Inimus himself was stunned that anyone could be such a blatant liar.

'It's not true. None of it's true,' he bellowed. But his voice could not be heard over the din of the crowd. He had no microphone.

The drums reached a shattering climax. The curtains were flung open – and a hundred thousand eyes were fixed gazing out of the darkness on to King Conger.

Inimus blinked, then instinctively went into his specially prepared routine. He roared and tried to crash his way out of the cage. To no avail, naturally.

'This mighty exhibit is our prisoner for life,' announced Ray Thornback. 'We will take him round the sea as a living example of prehistory.'

'No, no. You won't. You can't.'

'Prisoner for life?' yelled Inimus. 'That's not what I agreed.'

He roared and crashed against the cage. This time for real. But it was still no use. The cunning Thornback had foreseen what would happen and made sure the cage would contain his captive beast.

'The murdering liar,' shouted Art Hake. 'Let me at him.'

He swam out of the enclosure and made his way

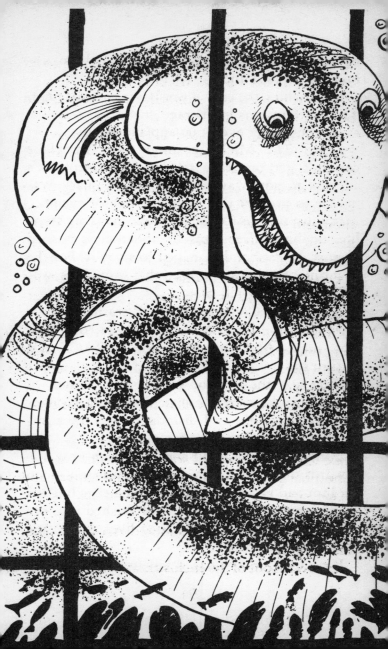

backstage, followed by Sanderson, whom no-body knew was there.

Meanwhile, the crowd was having a great time. The more Inimus in his rage crashed against the cage, the louder everyone applauded.

Mako The Micky ensured that Art Hake couldn't get on stage to disrupt Thornback's address in any way. But the fierce shark was unable to prevent the inevitable tide of events.

Inimus, furious for the first time in his big small life, unable to free himself, nonetheless pushed against the cage and managed to sway it. For the first time, the crowd realized that something was going wrong. It fell silent.

Again King Conger roared and crashed against the top of the cage. Again it swayed, this time even more. And there was a loud CRACK as a fixture split.

This was the cue for mass panic. Waves of hysteria broke over the crowd as King Conger used all his might and dislodged the cage com-pletely.

Inimus forced himself and his prison upwards towards the surface. But the strain was too much for him and he lost his balance. The cage hurtled downwards at great speed, and crashed into the auditorium. Fish swam for their lives as the cage smashed on impact.

King Conger was dazed but free.

15 · The Scales of Justice

The sudden realization that he was free plunged Inimus into the depths of confusion. What should he do now?

He felt lost and betrayed. If only Angel Sweet-lips would come and help him. All he wanted to do was to go home. He didn't enjoy being the centre of attention. He didn't enjoy being a star. Most of all, he didn't enjoy everyone being frightened of him.

Fortunately, Angel was *not* frightened of King Conger. As the crowd swam off in panic, she made her way up to Inimus as he sat confused in his open cage.

'Don't worry, Inimus,' she said in her most soothing voice. 'I'll go and find Rock and we'll get you back home.'

Meanwhile, backstage, Art Hake confronted Ray Thornback.

'Why, Ray? Why?' Hake looked genuinely upset.

'Oh, go and get filleted. You've no idea how to promote these things. You're too soft for this game. It's a cruel wet world we live in. You've got to take your chances while you can.'

'Is that what you said to Cecil Goldfish on the last night of his life? Is that why you killed him – because he wouldn't see things your way? Is that why you forged his signature on the letter of agreement which conned me into this project?'

'What are you talking about?' yelled Thornback.

Art Hake was in no mood to answer questions. Instead, he pulled out a gun and fired at Thornback. He missed. Thornback darted for cover.

He was about to fire again, but for the timely arrival of Rock Salmon, who deftly swam up behind Hake and flicked the gun out of his fin.

Hercule Poisson and his fish arrived on the scene, and managed to hold both Hake and Thornback.

'So what I want to know now, messieurs, is which of you killed Cecil Goldfish?'

Both fish gave the same answer: 'He did!'

There was a silence in the water, a silence which was broken by a small but sincere voice.

'Neither of them killed Cecil Goldfish, as it were. He's very much alive.'

'Then who's the fish we've got on the slab in the morgue?' asked Poisson.

'Hey, that's simple,' replied Rock Salmon. 'I mean, I seem to have spent quite a lot of time pretending to be my nephew Salmon Davis, haven't I?'

'Exactly, sir.'

'You mean Cecil Goldfish concocted this whole plan?' exclaimed Art Hake.

'That's right,' said Sanderson. 'Thornback knew Goldfish was still alive. He was in league with him the whole time. You see, Goldfish had huge debts. His death would wipe the slate clean, as it were. The expedition to the Precific Sea would be a huge success, and Thornback and Goldfish would clean up.'

'Is this true, Thornback?' asked Art Hake quietly.

'If it is, then where's the living proof? If Sam Goldfish isn't dead, then where is he?'

'This way, gentlefish, as it were.' Sanderson ushered them all out into the auditorium.

There was Inimus, curled up in a large ball at the bottom of the hall, apparently talking to himself.

'No. I can't, you see. I promised Sanderson I wouldn't, so that's that. No, I don't want your money. It's no use to me. I'm going home, you see and money hasn't been invented there yet. . . . Ah, there you all are. I guarded him just as you asked, Sanderson.'

Inimus unwound himself to reveal one live though somewhat frightened Cecil Goldfish.

'Great plan, Sam, I have to admit,' muttered Art Hake. 'You had us all fooled. Wetter luck next time.'

'We nearly got away with it,' said Ray Thornback.

'Ah well, that's show business,' agreed Goldfish as Poisson and the minions of the law took them off to the police station.

Epifish

Rock and Sanderson, accompanied by Angel Sweetlips and Professor October, escorted Inimus all the way to the Straits of Bad Luck.

They decided that, for security reasons, it would be best if the giant stayed in his cage. Although he was strictly non-violent, they didn't want to frighten all the fish they met on the way.

Angel spent some time with him inside the cage. The huge conger eel was quiet and thoughtful. Angel spent the time telling him about life in Atlantis.

'It's not all bad here in the future, Inimus.'

King Conger smiled, but said nothing.

They released him at the Straits, and said a short emotional goodbye.

Inimus swam off, then stopped. He turned back and looked straight at Angel.

'You know, I think I've learned something from this,' he said.

'What have you learned, Inimus?' asked Angel

with a smile.

'I've learned that I prefer to be a small fish in a big pond than the other way round.'

He turned and swam away.

'There's a moral in that somewhere,' suggested Sanderson.

'Come on,' said Rock, 'let's get back to the small pond. We've earned ourselves a rest.'

FIN

You can see more Magnet Paperbacks
on the following pages:

ROBERT LEE

Fishy Business

Rock Salmon, private detective, finds himself involved in the underwater gangland world of Atlantis when a priceless shell is stolen. Life becomes dangerous for Rock as he tangles with slippery characters like Ed Stingray and Ernst Fishfinger, and the whole business looks very fishy indeed . . .

An exciting and hilarious detective thriller set in the depths of the ocean.

SAM McBRATNEY

Zesty

10p a week to insure all your rulers, pens, pencils, dinner
tickets, break biscuits and sweets. It seemed like a good
idea. 10p a week against loss, theft or criminal damage. It
was a *brilliant* idea.

Mandy Taylor, Shorty, Gowso, Knuckles and Legweak
all thought so. But Penny Brown had her own ideas about
any scheme run by the dreadful Jimmy Zest. One –
nobody would get anything back; Zesty was too clever.
Two . . . IT WOULD GO WRONG.

MICHAEL GRATER

Alf Gorilla

Batty and his gang of rats need a minder. It's a dangerous world out there, full of cats and other enemies. The rats need protection – and find it in the shape of a kidnapped gorilla, things soon start getting out of hand . . .

A hairy and hilarious book.

ADRIAN HENRI

The Phantom Lollipop Lady and other poems

A sparkling collection of poems especially for children by one of Britain's best-known poets.

'A new collection of poems is like a box of assorted chocolates . . . Adrian Henri's new collection is a very tasty selection. Open this tempting book yourselves and pick out your best ones . . .' *Adèle Geras*

JEAN URE

Swings and Roundabouts

Drama school suits Jason down to the ground. There's lots of acting and dancing and a chance to show off. Then he gets his big break — an audition for a part in a television commercial. Jason's so sure he's done well that he tells all his friends the part's his. But there's a nasty shock ahead . . .

ANDREW MATTHEWS

Dixie's Demon

When your pet is small and a bit on the fiendish side, Dixie discovers, you get an awful lot of hassle. You get into trouble with your parents, your friends laugh at you and the biggest yobbo in the school wants to duff you up. Added to which, demons have some . . . well . . . peculiar personal habits.

A very funny story of one boy and his demon.

More Fiction from Magnet Books

While every effort is made to keep prices low, it is sometimes necessary to increase prices at short notice. Magnet books reserve the right to show new retail prices on covers which may differ from those previously advertised in the text or elsewhere.

The prices shown below were correct at the time of going to press.

All these books are available at your bookshop or newsagent, or can be ordered direct from the publisher. Just tick the titles you want and fill in the form below.

MAGNET BOOKS   Cash Sales Department
P.O. Box 11, Falmouth,
Cornwall TR10 9EN

...end cheque or postal order, no currency, for purchaser price quoted and the following for postage and packing;

K	60p for the first book, 25p for the second book and 15p for each additional book ordered to a maximum charge of £1.90.
BFPO and Eire	60p for the first book, 25p for the second book and 15p for each next seven books, thereafter 9p per book.
Overseas Customers	£1.25 for the first book, 75p for the second book and 28p for each subsequent title ordered.

NAME (Block letters) ....

ADDRESS ....

....